THOMAS & FRIENDS™

The Big Surprise

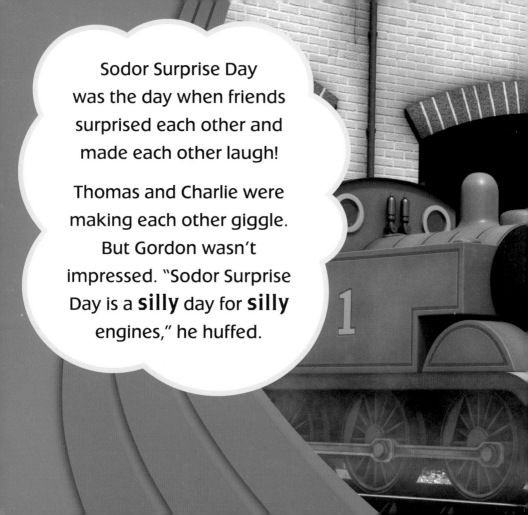

Sodor Surprise Day was the day when friends surprised each other and made each other laugh!

Thomas and Charlie were making each other giggle. But Gordon wasn't impressed. "Sodor Surprise Day is a **silly** day for **silly** engines," he huffed.

The Fat Controller arrived to tell them about a party that night at Callan Castle. He asked Thomas to collect the bunting from Maithwaite Station and Gordon to collect the fireworks from Brendam Docks.

Thomas wanted to surprise Gordon, so he hurried ahead to the Docks.

On the way Thomas stopped to talk to Rosie, who was pulling coal trucks. When Gordon came down the track, Thomas blew his whistle loudly.

PEEEP!

Rosie **jumped** in surprise, **bumping** into her trucks. Soot flew everywhere!

But Gordon wasn't surprised. He just **huffed** away.

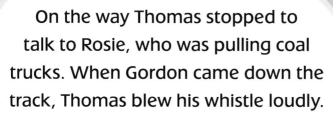

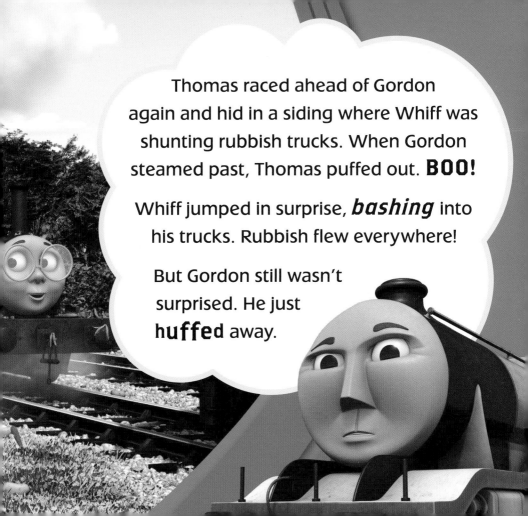

Thomas raced ahead of Gordon again and hid in a siding where Whiff was shunting rubbish trucks. When Gordon steamed past, Thomas puffed out. **BOO!**

Whiff jumped in surprise, *bashing* into his trucks. Rubbish flew everywhere!

But Gordon still wasn't surprised. He just **huffed** away.

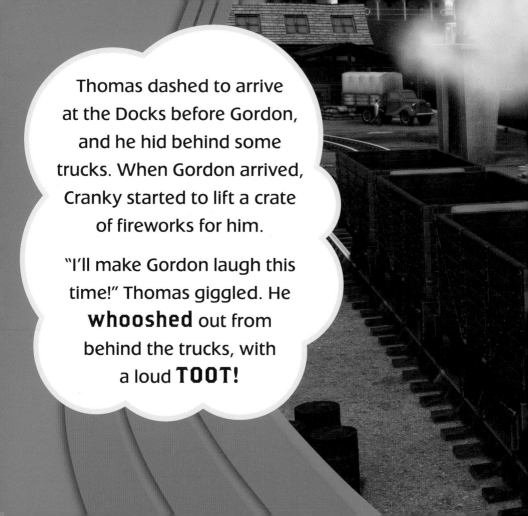

Thomas dashed to arrive at the Docks before Gordon, and he hid behind some trucks. When Gordon arrived, Cranky started to lift a crate of fireworks for him.

"I'll make Gordon laugh this time!" Thomas giggled. He **whooshed** out from behind the trucks, with a loud **TOOT!**

But Gordon still wasn't surprised. Gordon was cross.

"Your silly tricks didn't surprise me or make me laugh," Gordon said sternly to Thomas. "I told you Sodor Surprise Day was **silly**. Now I don't like it **at all**."

The Fat Controller arrived, looking **very stern** indeed.

"Thomas! There are no more fireworks for the party," he said. "And you haven't picked up the bunting. We will have to cancel the party!"

Thomas felt **terrible**. His silly pranks had ruined everything!

Then Thomas spotted Harold in the sky, and an idea flew into his funnel.

"Please don't cancel the party, Sir! I know how I can get Sodor Surprise Day back on track!" he said.

"Very well then," said The Fat Controller.

Gordon set off to pick up the bunting, and Thomas headed to the Washdown to get clean for the party. Whiff and Rosie were already there.

Once Thomas was clean, he puffed off to find Harold.

"Harold can help me save the day!" thought Thomas.

That night, Thomas steamed up to the party. Harold flew above him, decorated with **fairy lights!** It was a marvellous sight!

Gordon beamed. "I do like Sodor Surprise Day after all!" he laughed.

And Thomas was **so surprised**, he thought his boiler might burst!

PEEP! PEEP!

The End